ANTONIO'S APPRENTICESHIP

Painting a Fresco in Renaissance Italy

To Dr. and Mrs. Morrison

The Chapel of San Francesco at Castellino in Florence
and the characters in this book are fictitious.

Copyright © 1996 by Taylor Morrison
Printed in the United States of America
First Edition

Library of Congress Cataloging-in-Publication Data
Morrison, Taylor.
Antonio's apprenticeship : painting a fresco in Renaissance Italy
/ written and illustrated by Taylor Morrison. — 1st ed.
p.   cm.
Summary: An apprentice in fifteenth-century Italy tells about his
activities during the process of the painting of the frescoes in the
Chapel of San Francesco in Florence.
ISBN 0-8234-1213-X (hardcover : alk. paper)
1. Antonio, di Benedetto, 15th cent. — Juvenile literature.
2. Mural painting and decoration, Renaissance — Italy — Florence —
Juvenile literature.   3. Jesus Christ — Art — Juvenile literature.
4. Chapel of San Francisco (Castello, Florence, Italy) — Juvenile
literature.   [1. Antonio, di Benedetto, 15th cent.   2. Mural
Painting and decoration — Italy.   3. Painting, Renaissance — Italy.
4. Jesus Christ — Art.]   I. Title.
ND623.A625M67   1996   95-4871   CIP   AC
759.5 — dc20

ANTONIO'S APPRENTICESHIP

Painting a Fresco in Renaissance Italy

written and illustrated by

TAYLOR MORRISON

Holiday House/New York

This day of our Lord April 1, 1478 is a glorious one. My father has made arrangements for me to work as an apprentice in my uncle Charbone's successful paint shop. I wish to become a famous painter cherished by all of Italy.

Here is what my uncle wrote in his shop book:

> *I record that I, Charbone di Benedetto, have hired the said Antonio di Benedetto to be my apprentice in the art of painting for one year. Antonio must come to the shop any time that I wish, day or night. I will pay the said Antonio 12 florins in one year, and I will provide him with meals and a bed in my home.*

When I arrive in Florence, my uncle greets me in front of his studio. "Antonio, I am pleased that you safely made it to my shop," he says. He slaps me on the back with his big hand and guides me inside.

"Time to work, Antonio. Our glorious city is prospering and we have been blessed with several commissions."

My two cousins, Maso and Galgano, are also apprentices. Maso is painting decorations onto a cassone, a large chest, while Galgano is sketching Maso as he works. Charbone sits down before an altarpiece he is finishing. He calls to me, "Antonio, go and gather some dry willow branches to begin making charcoal sticks for drawing."

Every day, Charbone orders me to do more tedious chores. He makes me sand panels, prepare tinted paper, and put charcoal sticks in the oven.

One morning, I ask my uncle, "Why do you constantly ask me to prepare and make materials? I will not become a famous painter by gathering willow branches!"

"You will better understand how to draw and paint after you develop a deep knowledge of the materials," Charbone explains.

For the next few hours, I grudgingly continue to make brushes from goose feathers, sticks, and weasel hair. While I work, Charbone explains the contract he is reading. It is for a series of twenty-two frescoes, or large wall paintings. The contract has strict instructions: how much the patrons will pay, what the frescoes will illustrate, and when the series will be completed. The patrons want my uncle to paint pictures from the life of Christ on the walls of the Chapel of San Francesco at Castellino.

"Do you get many commissions?" I ask him.

"Yes," he answers. "I'm asked to do everything from painting portraits and altarpieces to decorating beds, shields, and even banners for festivals. You can see my work all over Florence."

"Do all those rules in the contract bother you?" I ask.

"No, Antonio. Painters show their greatness by working within the boundaries they are given."

"Are there many arguments over contracts?"

"Yes," he answers. "I occasionally argue with patrons about payment. Once, I exchanged blows with a foul-tempered painter who was competing for the same contract as I was."

"Who won the fight?" I ask.

"Enough questions," Charbone says. "We must get started on the frescoes today, since the masons have finished constructing our scaffolding. We will leave immediately and begin work this afternoon."

As we walk to Castellino on the other side of Florence, the bright sun warms my back. Finally, with this new commission, I will receive some relief from my boring studio chores.

We enter the cool, musty chapel, and Galgano climbs up the rickety ladder to the scaffolding. Looking down, he shouts, "The devil has pulled many unfortunate painters from their scaffolding, Antonio." Clutching the ladder tightly, I climb to the platform. I help Galgano check the wall for wet spots, since moisture destroys frescoes. With large brooms, we sweep the dirt and dust from the walls. We work until the sun sinks and the chimes of evening vespers tell us our workday is over.

The next morning, we mix two parts sand with one part lime and one part water, and allow it to sit for a day. Then we add small amounts of water to create a rough plaster called arriccio. Charbone loads a trowel with plaster and throws it onto the surface of the wall. When we finish a layer, Maso and I level the plaster with large boards. Before the next coat, we scratch a pattern onto the wet surface with small metal-toothed combs. The combed patterns create a good surface for the following layers of plaster.

By midday, I am exhausted and hungry, but Charbone has an errand for me.

"Go outside and track down a white pig. Its tail is the most magnificent for brushes."

I find a large, beautiful pig, but he tries to bite me and snorts off. I finally catch him and return to the chapel with a fistful of hog hair.

The wall grows to nearly four inches thick as we continue to apply layers of plaster. Now it is time to apply the final rough coat. When the plaster is level and has hardened a bit, Galgano hands me a large hog-hair brush soaked in water. He instructs me to splatter the water on the surface. Maso and Charbone follow right behind me, smoothing the wall with wooden trowels in a circular motion.

After I finish splattering, Charbone orders me to practice my drawing for a while. As I make my sketch, Charbone slaps my shoulder and says, "Brunelleschi did not invent perspective for you to butcher!" He takes my paper and corrects my drawing.

It is discouraging. I wonder if my uncle will ever find me worthy enough to work on my own designs.

As we walk home from Castellino, Charbone sends me to the pharmacist. He gives me a few florins to buy colored minerals for making paint.

Artisans and patrons walk from shop to shop through the crowds. They talk, laugh, and argue while the hammers of metal workers clang in the background.

Carpenters, sculptors, and painters share their skills for the sake of quality and speed. Uncle has drawn designs for the sculptor down the street. The carpenter around the corner often appears with wooden panels on which Charbone can paint. Apprentices from the goldsmith's shop visit to look at our work, and often boast that their meager drawings are better than our own.

When I return to the studio, Charbone shows me how to make color. He fills a lamp with linseed oil and says, "Let us start by making black." Lighting the lamp, he places the flame two fingers from the base of a baking dish. The flame causes a black soot to form on the bottom. He sweeps it off, and I put it into a jar labeled lampblack. Next Uncle instructs me to fetch a pail filled with a mixture of lime and water that has been soaking for a week. "I want you to make little cakes of the mixture and carry them up to the roof to dry in the sun," he explains.

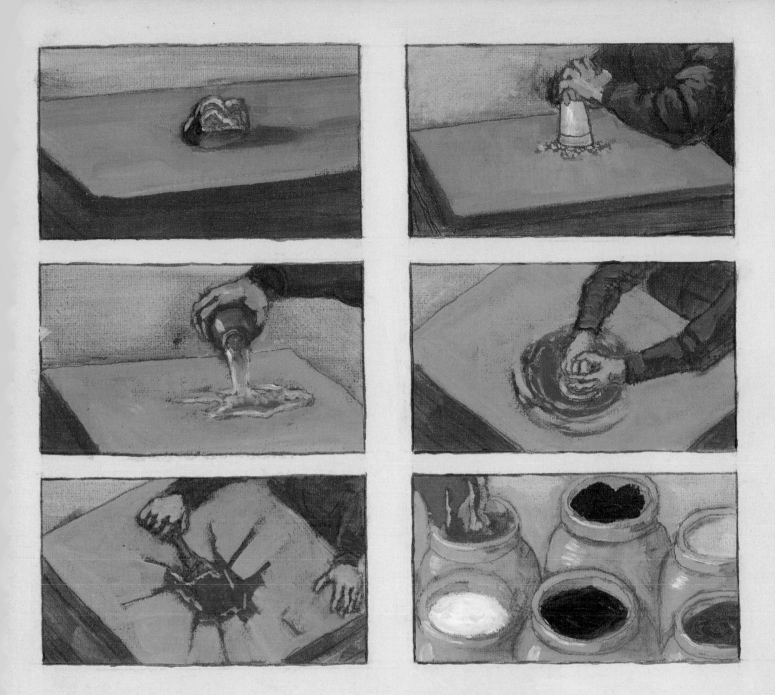

 While the cakes are drying, I return to the shop. I crush the minerals I bought at the pharmacist's and add water. Then I grind each mixture separately into pigment.

 As I scoop up the colors and place them in different jars, Maso warns me, "Label the colors clearly, since it is difficult to tell them apart in the shadows of a chapel."

The next day, my cousin, Tessa, comes to the studio. "It is time to prepare figure drawings for the fresco cycle," Charbone announces. "Tessa will pose as the Virgin Mary, then Antonio will follow as the angel Gabriel, and finally Galgano will dress as a shepherd."

After Charbone finishes his sketches, he selects the figure drawings he wants for making the frescoes. Galgano and I enlarge the drawings with grids so they will be big enough for the chapel walls. We poke tiny holes along the lines, because later these holes will allow us to transfer the drawings to the wall.

In a few days, we return to the Chapel of San Francesco. On the rough plaster, Charbone does a rapid charcoal sketch of the architecture and landscape. Next we add the figures. We use a technique called pouncing. With small pieces of wax, we attach the corners of the large figure drawings to the wall. We pat the drawings with bags of charcoal. The charcoal dust filters from the bags through the pricked holes in the drawings, making dotted outlines of the figures on the wall.

Charbone stares at the drawing for a long time. Occasionally he wipes off some of the lines, and with a piece of charcoal makes slight changes where he feels they need improvement. When Charbone is through making alterations, Maso uses a feather pen to apply red ink over the charcoal lines. Otherwise, the charcoal will rub off.

After so much preparation, it is time to paint the frescoes. Charbone asks Maso to help him work on the difficult figures.

Then he calls to me, "Antonio, help Galgano paint that rock, but do not make a slip or we will have to chip the wall out and lose a day's work."

Finally, Charbone is permitting me to use a brush instead of just ordering me to make one.

Charbone stares at the drawing for a long time. Occasionally he wipes off some of the lines, and with a piece of charcoal makes slight changes where he feels they need improvement. When Charbone is through making alterations, Maso uses a feather pen to apply red ink over the charcoal lines. Otherwise, the charcoal will rub off.

After so much preparation, it is time to paint the frescoes. Charbone asks Maso to help him work on the difficult figures.

Then he calls to me, "Antonio, help Galgano paint that rock, but do not make a slip or we will have to chip the wall out and lose a day's work."

Finally, Charbone is permitting me to use a brush instead of just ordering me to make one.

"The walls are alive with fresco!" says Charbone. "It is born in the morning when the plaster is laid and dies at night when it dries."

The church wall develops into a giant puzzle of plaster pieces.

In the mornings that follow, we lay a patch of smooth plaster, or intonaco, over the arriccio or rough plaster we applied earlier. This patch covers the red ink drawing underneath. Next we must repounce the drawing so it is visible on the fresh plaster. After this is done, Charbone uses a goose-feather brush to ink over the charcoal dots.

With a cup of green ink, Charbone adds shadows to the face. He gently lays down washes of color, one over the other, as the face develops. Pausing after each wash, he waits for the pigment to sink into the plaster. When he has finished the head and the plaster begins to harden, Charbone stops painting. Maso grabs a sharp knife and neatly trims away the excess intonaco, creating a nice, clean edge. Tomorrow, we will trowel on a new piece of intonaco next to the piece we finished today. Eventually the whole surface will be covered.

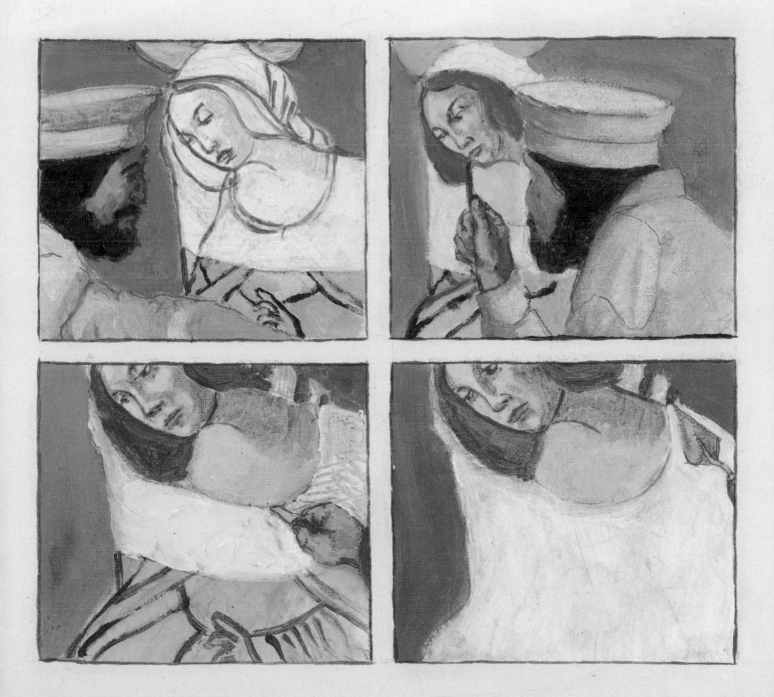

These months of fresco painting are the most exciting and exhausting of my life. It is a challenge to make the wall come alive. I struggle to imitate Charbone's technique so the frescoes will look as if they were painted by one hand.

When the sun is low, my uncle gathers us together and reminds us: "One must have the skill to be a good painter, but also maintain strong family relations, constant religious practice, an active role in our guild, and a smart business sense. These are the essential parts of being a painter."

At last, the frescoes are ready for all of Florence to see. Charbone's patrons are delighted with our handsome frescoes. I am proud to be an apprentice to my master Charbone and of the work we have created for our fellow Florentines.

GLOSSARY

altarpiece: A painting that decorates the space above and behind the altar of a church.

apprentice: Someone who is learning an art or trade by working for a skilled worker.

arriccio: The rough first coat of plaster in fresco painting.

artisan: Someone who is trained in a trade such as carpentry, sculpture, or painting.

Brunelleschi, Filippo (1377–1446): A famous architect of the Italian Renaissance. Also a great mathematician, he invented linear perspective.

cassone: A large decorated chest.

commission: An art project assigned to an artisan and paid for by a patron.

contract: A written agreement between an artist and patron spelling out the rules of a commission.

florin: A gold coin used in Florence during the Renaissance.

fresco: The art of painting on moist plaster with water-based pigments.

gesso: A white paste painted on a panel to create a good painting surface.

goldsmith: An artisan who creates and sells objects of gold.

grid: A network of squares of equal size used to enlarge small drawings but without changing the proportions.

intonaco: The final smooth layer of plaster in fresco painting.

linseed oil: A yellow oil made from flaxseed, used to make black pigment.

patron: An individual or group that pays an artist to do a work of art.

pigment: Colored powder that is mixed with water to make paint.

plaster: A pastelike mixture of sand, lime, and water that hardens when applied to a wall or ceiling.

pounce: To pat charcoal on a pricked drawing in order to transfer it to another surface.

Renaissance: Meaning "rebirth" or "revival," it was a period of history beginning in the 14th century and lasting into the 17th. During the Renaissance, there was a revival of interest in classical art, architecture, and philosophy.

scaffolding: A temporary structure built of timbers and planks that painters use when working in high places.

trowel: A hand-held tool used to apply and smooth plaster on a wall.

vespers: A service of evening worship when church bells are rung.